SHIP'S COOK GINGER
and
TIM'S LAST VOYAGE

Red Fox

SHIP'S COOK GINGER

ANOTHER TIM STORY

by

Edward Ardizzone

ALSO BY EDWARD ARDIZZONE
PUBLISHED BY RED FOX:

Diana and her Rhinoceros

A Red Fox Book. Published by Random House Children's Books,
20 Vauxhall Bridge Road, London SW1V 2SA. A division of Random
House UK Ltd. London Melbourne Sydney Auckland Johannesburg and
agencies throughout the world.

Ship's Cook Ginger first published in 1977 by The Bodley Head
Ltd. Text and illustrations © Edward Ardizzone 1977.

Tim's Last Voyage first published in 1972 by The Bodley Head Ltd.
Text and illustrations © Edward Ardizzone 1972.

This Red Fox edition first published in 1993.
All rights reserved.
Printed and bound in Hong Kong

RANDOM HOUSE UK Limited Reg. No. 954009

ISBN 0 09 916401 9

It was holiday time and Tim and Ginger, who lived by the sea, were bored.

There was no one on the beach to play with and not even the old boatman to talk to.

'Let's run away to sea again,' said Ginger crossly, but Tim said that he couldn't because he had promised his mother not to.

'Oh, poof! You and your silly old promises,' shouted Ginger more crossly than before.

Tim's mother noticed that Tim looked pale, mooched about and would not finish his dinner, so she went to the chemist and bought a big bottle of tonic. The chemist said it was the best tonic he had. It was especially good for boys because it was so nasty that they hurried up and became better.

And, my word, it was nasty. Poor Tim had to take three large spoonfuls of it a day.

But in spite of this he mooched about more and more, became paler and paler, ate less and less of his dinner and even began to get thinner.

Tim's father said that he knew what was wrong with Tim, that tonics would not help. The boy was pining for the open sea.

Why not ask Captain McFee to take them all for a voyage in his new ship? Ginger of course must come too.

Tim's mother did not like the idea at all. Something horrid always happened when Tim and Ginger went to sea. Tim's father said, 'Nonsense, my dear. This time we will be with them which makes all the difference.' But Tim's mother was still worried and she was right.

The next day they walked to the docks where they found Captain McFee in his ship *Claribel*.

Captain McFee said that he was sailing in three days' time for the Northern Isles and would be pleased to take them with him. He had a nice cabin for Tim's father and mother, but the boys would have to work and live with the crew.

You can just imagine how excited were Tim and Ginger as they packed and helped to get everything ready for the voyage. The only person who sometimes looked sad was Tim's mother.

The cat was sad too because he was going to be left behind.

However, when they arrived on board the *Claribel* and Tim's mother saw their cabin she felt much happier. It was beautiful.

Tim's job was to stay on the bridge and help the Captain by doing such things as running messages and fetching the Captain his tea.

Ginger, who was not so clever, had to help the second mate. He had to paint and scrub and do other kinds of work.

Unfortunately he was sometimes idle and would hide in a boat and read comics instead of getting on with the job. This made him un-popular with the second mate who did not like boys anyhow and who was often nasty to him.

For the first few days the weather was lovely.
The sky was blue, the sea was blue and the little
waves danced and sparkled in the sun.

Tim's father and mother sat in deck chairs in
the sun and were having a lovely restful holiday.

Tim enjoyed working for the Captain and even Ginger did not mind scrubbing decks in the nice bright warm weather.

Best of all the ship's cook was a very good cook and made the most scrumptious meat pies.

THEN THE BLOW FELL...

One day Sparks the wireless officer asked Tim to take a message to his father.

When his father read it he was horrified. 'Something dreadful has happened at the office,' he said. 'We must all go home at once or we will be ruined.'

Captain McFee was very kind and said that
he would put them on shore at the nearest port
where they could get a train home, but he would
like the boys to stay with him as he found them
very useful. Tim's mother did not like this a bit
and said 'NO'.

Tim and Ginger begged and begged her to let them stay. At last she said yes, though she was very unhappy about it.

The Captain gave Tim and Ginger leave to go to the station and see Tim's parents off, but he said that they must be back on board by nine o'clock as the *Claribel* sailed then. This left plenty

of time for the boys to have a lovely meal of fish and chips, with ices to follow.

In fact, when they arrived on board they were too full to eat even a tiny bit of the cook's scrumptious meat pie, which, as you will find out later, was lucky for them.

When Tim went up to the bridge next morning he was happy to find that the *Claribel* was now at sea and out of sight of land, but he was unhappy to find the Captain looking ill and the man at the wheel not much better.

All the Captain could say was, 'Get me some tea. I feel awful.'

Tim dashed down to the galley. There he found the cook lying on the floor. When the cook saw Tim he gave a groan and said, 'Don't eat the pie,' and fainted away.

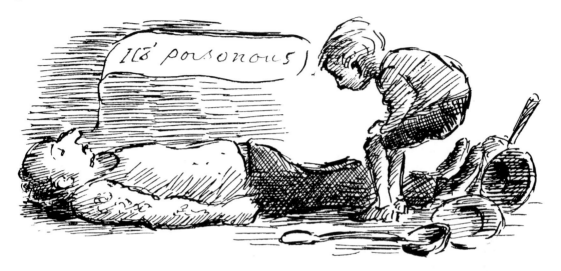

Then Tim ran to the wireless cabin to find Sparks also lying on the floor. Sparks whispered a message before he fainted.

Back on the bridge again Tim found the second mate standing by the wheel. Captain McFee had fainted away and the sailor was groaning on the deck.

'Boy,' said the second mate, 'the first mate is sick, as well as half the crew. I am now in command of this ship. We will wait here for a relief ship to take the sick to a hospital on shore. Then we will go on with the voyage. But remember we now have only half a crew, so you boys will have to work twice as hard.

'Ginger tells me he is a good cook, so I have made him ship's cook.'

By the time the relief ship had arrived, the wind blew harder and the waves were too big for the ships to float side by side, so the sick men had to be taken to the relief ship in boats; a long and dangerous task.

Tim's job was to look after the sick men as his boat went backwards and forwards between the ships. Ginger was kept in the galley cooking a hot meal for tired men.

And the crew of the *Claribel* were indeed tired as they settled down to what they hoped would be a lovely hot meal. But it was horrible. It was a stew and the bosun found a mouse in his portion. Ginger was very unpopular.

Poor Tim, like all the others, could not eat his stew and was so hungry and so tired that he longed to go to sleep in his bunk. But this was not to be. The second mate called for him to go to the bridge.

The engines had now been started and the ship moved forward in the teeth of a gale. Big waves and driving rain made it difficult to see ahead.

The mate ordered Tim to take the wheel from Seaman Bloggs who was tired, and to steer North and keep a sharp lookout.

'But, sir,' said Tim, 'Captain McFee said we must steer East to avoid the Black Cape and its deadly rocks.'

'What!' roared the mate. 'Question my orders? Be off with you. I will deal with you in the morning.'

Sadly Tim crept into his bunk. He was frightened because he knew he was right.

Poor Tim could not sleep, he could only wonder how to save the ship and possibly their lives. At last he said to himself, 'I must tell the bosun.'

'You are right, my boy,' said the bosun. 'We should travel East but it is no good telling the mate, he would only be angry. We must have a plan, but we have some days to spare, so go to bed and sleep.'

The next few days were horrible for all. Ginger's cooking became worse than ever. He put, by mistake, sugar in the soup and salt in the custard. He even put mustard in the coffee to make it taste warmer and his sandwiches of bread and raspberry jam with a sardine in the middle were the nastiest of the lot.

Poor Tim had a horrible time too. As they were short of crew he had to spend many hours at the wheel. The bosun's plan was that Tim should steer to the East every time the mate was not looking, and if he was caught out to make excuses.

Excuses such as—

'There was a trawler on the port bow.'

'I had to avoid a whale.'

'A coastal steamer was passing in shore of us.'

But all the time Tim was worried because he was not sure that the mate believed him and, worse still, because he was not sure if he had steered the ship enough to the East to avoid the deadly rocks ahead.

The next morning he was to know.

It was early when Tim heard sailors shouting, 'Rocks ahead!' and rushed to the bridge. There he found the bosun and the mate.

Looking ahead he could just see the Black

Cape and a line of terrible rocks with waves
breaking over them.

The mate was too frightened to do anything
but tremble. The bosun took charge.

The bosun told Tim to take the wheel, while he went on deck to get the men to collect planks and ropes to make some sort of raft, should the worst happen and the *Claribel* get smashed on the rocks.

Tim did his best to steer clear of the rock he saw ahead, but it got nearer and nearer all the time. From outside he could hear the sound of the waves and of men shouting. From inside only the terrible chattering of the mate's teeth. He was shivering with fear.

Then the miracle happened. The *Claribel* had almost struck the rock when an extra big wave lifted her past it. The rock was the outermost rock so the *Claribel* was now safe in open water.

A great cheer came from the men on deck. Many ran up to the bridge to shake Tim's hand and cry out, 'You've saved us. Your steering has saved us.'

From here it was only a short way to the next port. Soon they were inside the little harbour. On the quay was Captain McFee and with him all the crew they had left behind. They were quite well now.

Once on board Captain McFee soon heard

about the *Claribel*'s narrow escape and asked the mate how it had happened. The mate said that it was all Tim's fault for not obeying his orders.

The Captain looked at Tim with a sad stern face, but poor Tim could say nothing. After all he had disobeyed orders, though it was to save the ship.

The bosun and some of the crew standing nearby heard what was said and, not wanting Tim to be blamed, told the Captain the whole story.

Upon which the Captain turned on the mate in fury and called him—

        a liar

        a coward

        a poltroon

        a bad sailor

and lots of other horrible names and then dismissed him the ship.

On the voyage home the *Claribel* was a happy ship. The weather was fine, the old cook was back so the crew had delicious meals to eat, there were enough sailors on board so nobody had to work too hard, and the horrid second mate was not there to be beastly.

Captain McFee was particularly nice to Tim.
He taught him how to guide a ship by the sun
and stars and other things called the Art of Navi-
gation.

The cook was rather sorry for Ginger and being
a kind man he arranged for Ginger to help him
in the galley.

There he taught Ginger how to roast meat,
make stews, cook vegetables, also make pastry
and lots of delicious puddings.

Ginger really worked hard, did not answer back and learnt to cook quite well. His scrumptious pies were nearly as good as the cook's.

TIM'S LAST VOYAGE

by
EDWARD ARDIZZONE

To all my grandchildren

A gale was blowing. It was night. Tim, who lived in a house by the sea, could hear the waves crashing on the beach. He could not sleep. He loved the sea and longed to be in some small ship battling with the storm.

The next morning Tim and his friends Ginger and Charlotte walked down to the beach. The gale was blowing harder than ever. The waves were enormous and the three of them had lots of fun racing the waves as they rushed up the shingle beach.

Sometimes Ginger was foolish and would nearly get caught.

Then they climbed the steep shingle bank to talk to the old boatman.

'It is bad, bad!' said the boatman. 'See that line of white foam far out to sea? That is where even bigger waves are breaking in the shallow water of the Goodwin Sands. I will bet my bottom dollar there will be some poor ship

wrecked on those treacherous sands before the month is out.'

'Oh poof!' said Ginger. 'I've seen worse storms than this.'

After leaving the boatman they walked to the harbour nearby.

There, lying beside the quay, was a small steamer with a tall rusty red funnel. It was called the S.S. *Arabella*.

What a lovely name thought Tim, saying, 'Arabella, Arabella' over and over again to himself.

Hanging on the side of the ship was a notice on which was written 'WANTED DECK HANDS for short VOYAGE 3 DAYS ONLY.'

'Oh!' said Tim. 'How I wish we could get that job, but my father and mother would not like it.'

But Ginger only answered 'Poof! It's holiday time. The job is only for three days. They won't mind.'

Then they all climbed on board and met the mate who told them that as the ship was due to sail soon and as no men had applied for the job he would give it to Tim and Ginger. But he warned them that the work was hard and that the bosun was a tartar.

Tim told Charlotte to run home and tell his parents that he and Ginger would be away for three days. Then they went below to find the bosun and learn what jobs they had to do.

The bosun was indeed a tartar. 'What! Two snippets like you?' he shouted. 'I will work your fingers to the bone. See the carpenter, get pails and scrubbing brushes and, if I catch either of you idling, I will beat him with a rope's end.'

Joey Adze the ship's carpenter, handyman and storesman looked at them over his spectacles.

'Well! Well! Well! You are pretty small aren't

you!' he said. 'Here are brushes, pails and mops. Do the best you can and avoid the bosun, he's a TARTAR.'

Tim and Ginger were hard at work scrubbing out the saloon when the *Arabella* left port. At once she felt the force of the gale and rolled and pitched, which made Tim and Ginger's work harder still.

The bosun never allowed them to rest so they were two very tired little boys when they handed back their pails and brushes to Joey.

'You do look tired,' said Joey. 'I can see that the bosun has been a TARTAR as usual. Come dry your eyes, Ginger, and both of you make yourselves as comfortable as possible and rest.'

After they had rested for a little, Joey asked if either of them could read. When Tim said yes he gave him a book and said 'Read it to me.' The book was called *Moby Dick*. It was about a white whale.

'I was a whaler once,' said Joey. 'I have seen a white whale. It was a brute.'

Because it was so rough the *Arabella* could not get into the small port which was its destination. Instead it steamed south into the gale.

These were hard days; for the Captain who could not leave the bridge; for the mate who had to see that everything was shipshape; for Gino the cook because it was difficult to cook in rough weather; for Joey patching and mending; and for Tim and Ginger because the bosun with his rope's end made them work all day long, not caring if they were cold, wet and tired.

On the fourth day out a terrible thing happened. A great wave dashed over the side and washed the funnel overboard.

Water poured into the engine room. The engines stopped and the *Arabella* rolled like a dead thing in a waste of waters.

McAndrew the engineer came up from below saying that he could not start the engine again but would do his best.

The bosun, when he heard the news, cried out 'It's a doomed ship!' and shut himself in his

cabin with a bottle of rum. You see he was a
coward as well as a bully.

Ginger was frightened and sat huddled in a
corner of the galley. Gino tried to cheer him up
with tit bits of food.

For what seemed many days the helpless ship was blown to the north by the gale.

The Captain was worried because, as he could not see the sun by day nor the stars by night, he did not know where they were.

The mate was worried because there was three foot of water in the hold and still more coming on board.

The engineer was worried because he could not get the engines to start nor the pumps to work.

Gino was worried because he could not cook hot food for the crew and poor Ginger could not be comforted. But Ginger did try hard not to be so frightened and to help Gino cut bread and cheese.

The bosun only howled and shouted 'It's a doomed ship!' and drank more rum. This upset other members of the crew when they heard him.

All this time Tim and Joey sat stitching a great
sail to go on the foremast and help steady the
ship. When Tim's fingers became too sore to go

on stitching he would wedge himself into a corner and read *Moby Dick* to Joey. This made them both feel happier.

At last the sail was finished and with the help of the mate and some of the crew they ran it up the foremast. The wind filled it, the ship was steadier and less water came on board.

But, all the same, the gale drove them northward even faster than before and the Captain was

even more worried because he still
did not know where they were.

On to the north they went until one day there
was a grinding crash. The poor *Arabella* bounced
and shuddered to a stop. She had run aground

and was at the mercy of the breaking waves which dashed over her and carried away her boats and ventilators.

The Captain was very brave and very calm. He called the crew on deck. 'Men,' he said, 'this looks like the end of my dear ship *Arabella* and

it might be the end of us too. In a sea like this the ship will break up soon. Our boats are gone. Collect all the wood you can and make rafts so you can float ashore. But I do wish I knew where we were.'

At that moment there was a rift in the clouds
and the sun shone through. Tim saw a distant
beach and a house behind it. It was his house.
'Sir,' he shouted to the Captain, 'I can see my

house. We must be on the Goodwin Sands. The old boatman is sure to see us and tell the life-boatmen.' 'Good, but they must hurry,' answered the Captain, 'as we are sinking fast.'

Tim was right. The old boatman had seen them and told the lifeboatmen. The lifeboat, a grand new one with an engine, arrived just in time to save them all before the *Arabella* sank beneath the boiling foam.

Even now, if the weather is fine and the tide is low and you are standing on Tim's shingle beach looking far out to sea, you will make out two masts sticking up above the shallow waters of those treacherous sands. They are the *Arabella*'s.

Once in the lifeboat the bosun felt safe and became his old bullying self again. He said he would beat the boys with his rope's end if they would not sit still.

As for Ginger, when somebody said 'You

were frightened, weren't you?', he answered 'Poof! I was very brave helping Gino in the galley.' Gino said that Ginger had tried hard not to be frightened and was quite a help, which pleased Tim a lot.

Standing on the beach to watch the arrival of the lifeboat were Tim's father and mother and Charlotte. They were very surprised to see Tim and Ginger as they had no idea that the wrecked ship was the *Arabella*. They gave them a great welcome.

When all the hugging and kissing was over, Tim's mother made him promise not to go to sea again until he was grown up. Tim kept his promise.

But, when he was quite grown up he did go to sea and in time became a very fine sailor and the Captain of a great ship.

However he always remembered the time when he had been a little boy in a ship, so he was never unkind to his cabin boys and never beat them with a rope's end.